Luke Skywalker has vanished. In his absence, the sinister FIRST ORDER has risen from the ashes of the Empire and will not rest until Skywalker, the last Jedi, has been destroyed.

With the support of the REPUBLIC, General Leia Organa leads a brave RESISTANCE. She is desperate to find her brother, Luke, and gain his help in restoring peace and justice to the galaxy.

Leia has sent her most daring pilot on a secret mission to Jakku, where an old ally has discovered a clue to Luke's whereabouts . . . .

"THIS WILL BEGIN TO SET THINGS RIGHT,"

Lor San Tekka said as he handed Poe the data files that contained the map. "Without the Jedi, there can be no balance in the Force."

Just as Poe thanked Lor, a small round droid rolled into the hut where they were meeting, beeping frantically. It was BB-8, and he had urgent news!

The First Order had discovered Poe's mission. They had sent a platoon

POE DAMERON
An ace pilot, Poe Dameron is a leader in the Resistance's fight against the evil First Order. He soars into battle behind the controls of a modern X-wing fighter.

of stormtroopers to capture Poe and take the precious map. Already, they could hear the hum of ships landing at the edge of the village.

"You need to hide," Poe told the old man.

"You need to leave," Lor said.

Poe and BB-8 bolted back towards Poe's waiting ship.

Meanwhile, wave after wave of First Order stormtroopers attacked the village. The soldiers were dressed in identical white armour. As the villagers looked at the advancing army, they saw only a synchronised force of destruction.

But one stormtrooper was very different from his fellow soldiers. While the other troopers rushed to attack the village, he only pretended to fire at the civilians.

That stormtrooper was known as FN-2187. It was his first battle, but as he observed the chaos that surrounded him, he hoped it would be his last.

Over the sound of the attack, FN-2187 heard the rumble of a large shuttle craft. That could mean only one thing: Kylo Ren was there. FN-2187 knew that whatever the First Order was looking for on that planet, it must be important if Kylo was attending to it personally.

STORMTROOPERS
Equipped with sleek armour and powerful weapons, the stormtroopers enforce the will of the First Order.

Back at his X-wing fighter, Poe needed to get BB-8 and the map to safety. But the stormtroopers had damaged his ship beyond repair.

Poe knew he had no choice. He pulled out the map and gave it to BB-8.

"Get as far away from here as you can," Poe said. "I'll come back for you."

As BB-8 rolled away, Poe ran towards the burning village to see if he could help.

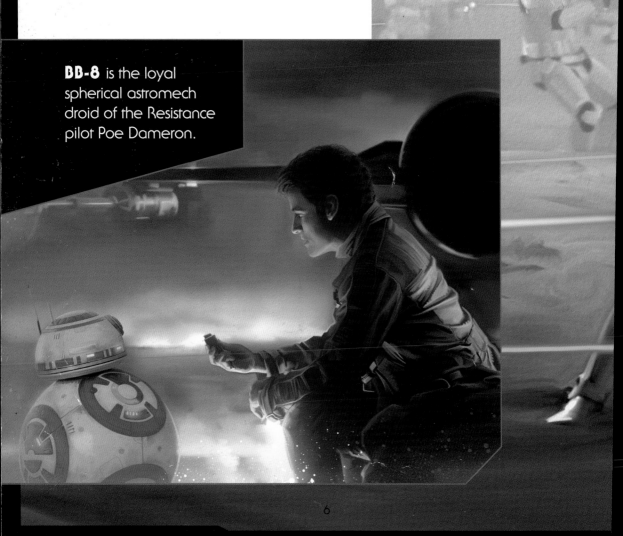

BB-8 is the loyal spherical astromech droid of the Resistance pilot Poe Dameron.

KYLO REN

A dark warrior strong with the Force, Kylo Ren commands First Order missions with a temper as fiery as his unconventional lightsaber.

What Poe saw there stopped him dead in his tracks. Kylo Ren had found Lor San Tekka.

"You know what I've come for," Kylo told the old man.

"I know where you come *from*. Before you called yourself Kylo Ren," Lor replied.

But Kylo was not in the mood for old remembrances.

"Give it to me," he snarled.

Lor refused to give up the location of the map. Seeing that Lor could not be persuaded, Kylo drew his lightsaber.

Poe saw what was coming and tried to fire his blaster at Kylo. But he couldn't save Lor. Kylo Ren used the Force to deflect Poe's attack and captured the Resistance pilot.

Kylo and the stormtroopers took Poe back to their massive Star Destroyer. On board, FN-2187 removed his helmet and started putting away his gear.

"FN-2187," someone said from behind him. "Submit your blaster for inspection."

He turned around to see his commanding officer, Captain Phasma. She must have noticed that he wasn't firing on the villagers.

The stormtrooper gave her his blaster and saluted. He knew once she ran a scan on his weapon, she would find out there was nothing wrong with it. It was only a matter of time until he was punished for disobeying orders.

FN-2187 was ready to leave the First Order behind him. But he'd need a pilot to help him escape . . .

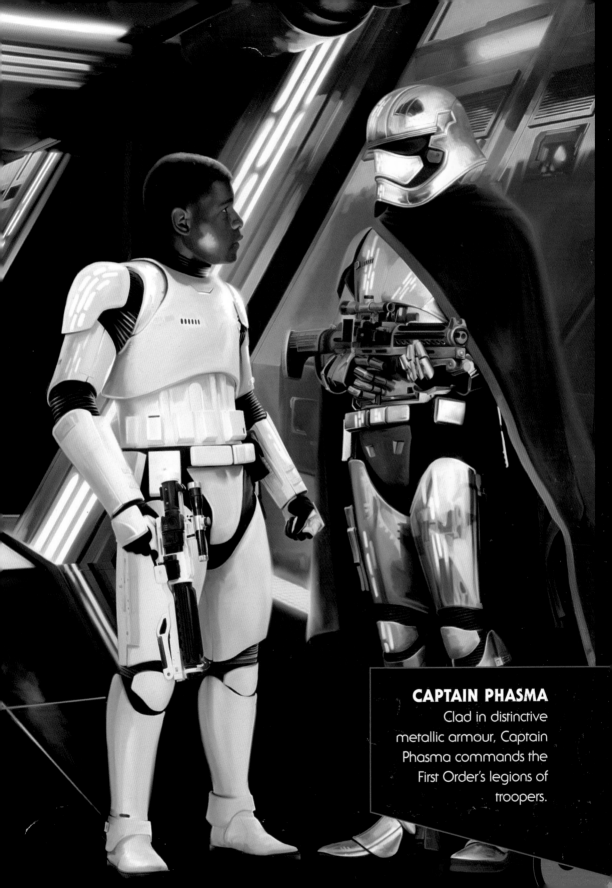

CAPTAIN PHASMA
Clad in distinctive metallic armour, Captain Phasma commands the First Order's legions of troopers.

Far away from the First Order and its evil plans,
a lone figure stood on the sandy surface of Jakku.

The scavenger was in the middle of a field of crashed ships and
abandoned military gear that stretched as far as the eye could see.
Methodically, she searched through the wreckage, looking for anything
she could sell at nearby Niima Outpost.

The scavenger's name was Rey. That name was one of the only clues she had to her past. Rey had been left on Jakku as a child, and she barely remembered her family or anything from before her life scrounging for food and shelter.

The fierce sun beat down on the scavenger's head. She had found only a few useful parts that day – barely enough to trade for dinner. But with the temperature rising across the desert plains, she couldn't afford to stay out in the heat much longer.

Rey carried her salvage to her speeder and set off for the outpost.

REY'S SPEEDER For quick transportation across the junk-strewn dunes of Jakku, Rey relies on her old salvaged speeder.

The Niima marketplace was alive with the hustle and bustle of trade. Booth after booth of merchants offered everything buyers could want, including used droids, spare speeder parts, and even expensive desert survival gear.

Rey caught a whiff of freshly cooked bloggin for sale, and her stomach rumbled.

Rey quickly made her way to Unkar Plutt's booth to sell what she had found that day. She hoped the old alien would give her a good bargain, but Unkar was not known for being generous – or even fair.

Sure enough, when Rey placed the spare parts before Unkar, he laughed. "Today, you get one . . . quarter portion."

Rey knew Unkar was cheating her. But after a long day, which had been part of a long month, which had been part of a long life on Jakku, Rey simply nodded and took the tiny food packet.

Rey hopped on her speeder and flew home.

For Rey, home was inside the wreckage of an old Imperial walker. She assumed the walker, along with all the crashed ships found on Jakku, must have been part of a battle long before.

Inside, Rey began eating her dinner, savouring every last bit of food. She could never be sure when she would get her next meal.

But as Rey sat in the stillness of her home, the silence was broken by a frantic beeping. It sounded like a droid – a droid in trouble.

Rey ran outside and towards the noise.

TEEDOS are small, brutish scavengers who roam Jakku's vast wasteland on their semi-mechanical luggabeasts.

Rey ran over a ridge and saw a little round droid trapped in a net.

The net was being dragged by an angry Teedo riding a huge luggabeast. Teedos often roamed the desert, looking for weak travellers to steal from. But Rey had never seen a droid travelling alone like that.

LUGGABEAST Beasts of burden found on frontier worlds, luggabeasts are semi-mechanical creatures whose faces are always hidden behind heavy armour plating.

She knew she had to help, so she called out to the Teedo to stop hurting the droid. The Teedo just shouted back angrily.

Rey, however, was not about to back down. She raised her staff menacingly, ready for a fight.

But the Teedo didn't attack Rey. He just kept shouting empty threats at her.

Unimpressed, Rey walked over to the droid and began cutting him out of the net.

The Teedo could see that keeping the droid would be more trouble than it was worth. He rode away from the pair, still shouting back at them.

Now that the droid was free, Rey looked down at him curiously.

"Where'd you come from?" she asked.

The droid beeped in response.

"Oh. *Classified*. Really? Well, me too," Rey teased. "Big secret."

Rey showed the droid how to get to Niima Outpost, then started walking home.

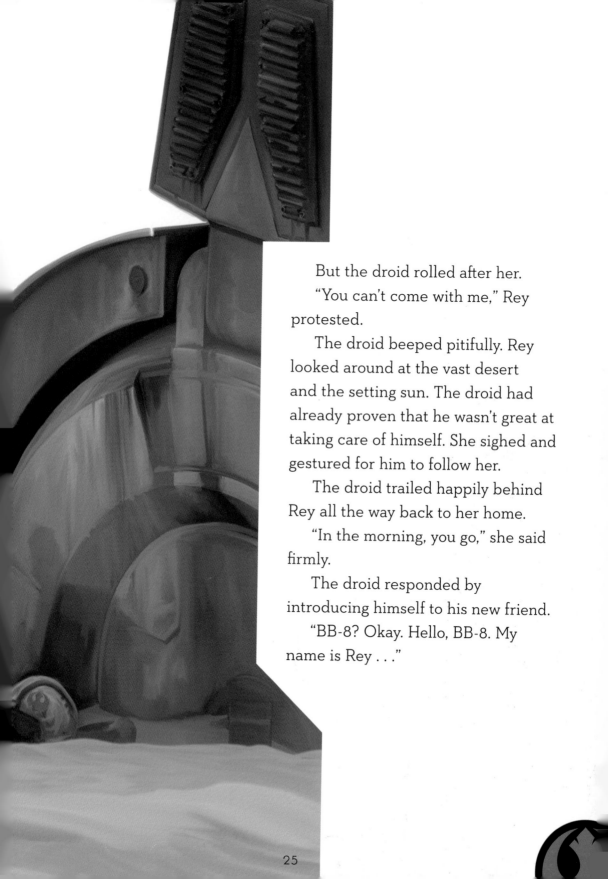

But the droid rolled after her.

"You can't come with me," Rey protested.

The droid beeped pitifully. Rey looked around at the vast desert and the setting sun. The droid had already proven that he wasn't great at taking care of himself. She sighed and gestured for him to follow her.

The droid trailed happily behind Rey all the way back to her home.

"In the morning, you go," she said firmly.

The droid responded by introducing himself to his new friend.

"BB-8? Okay. Hello, BB-8. My name is Rey . . ."

The next morning, Rey took BB-8 to Niima Outpost.

"There's a trader in bay three, might be able to give you a lift wherever you're going." Rey pointed to the busy landing paddock. "So . . . goodbye."

But once again, BB-8 refused to leave Rey's side. No matter what she said, BB-8 insisted that he stay with her.

Tired of arguing with the little droid, Rey decided to go about her business at the outpost while BB-8 tagged along.

Rey had picked up a few more spare parts on the way to the outpost, so she took them to Unkar Plutt's. Unkar wasn't very interested in Rey's salvage . . . but he was interested in BB-8. Unkar had heard the First Order was looking for a round white-and-orange droid that looked just like BB-8.

"What about the droid?" Unkar asked. "I'll pay for him."

"How much?" Rey asked before she could stop herself.

"Sixty portions," the alien replied.

Rey was shocked. That was more food than
she had ever seen in her life. But when she looked
down at BB-8, she knew what she had to do.

"The droid is not for sale," she replied.

Unkar was not happy. But that didn't bother Rey. She and
BB-8 simply walked away, heading back through the market.

Meanwhile, Kylo Ren was torturing Poe aboard his ship, hoping to extract any information about the map and the Resistance's plans.

Poe was in so much pain that he had told Kylo about BB-8.
But he had managed to keep the location of the Resistance base a secret.

As Kylo left Poe tied up in his cell, Poe worried that he wouldn't be able to resist the First Order enforcer much longer.

Hours passed.

Poe dreaded the moment Kylo would return.

Finally, the cell door opened, and a stormtrooper stepped inside.

"Kylo Ren wants the prisoner," the soldier said.

The stormtrooper led Poe from the cell, then removed his helmet. It was FN-2187!

"Listen carefully," the stormtrooper said. "I'm helping you escape. Can you fly a TIE fighter?"

Poe was stunned but quickly recovered.

"I can fly anything," he said confidently.

The pair ran to the hangar where all the ships were kept. FN-2187 spotted a Special Forces TIE fighter and took Poe to the cockpit.

"I always wanted to fly one of these things," Poe said. Quickly, he powered up the engine and flew them into space.

But the First Order wasn't going to let them get away that easily! The Star Destroyer fired on the escaping TIE fighter.

FN-2187 fired back and took out an entire line of cannons.

Poe started to cheer for his new friend, but then he realised they had yet to introduce themselves.

"I'm Poe Dameron. What's your name?"

"FN-2187!" the stormtrooper replied.

Poe thought the soldier deserved a better name than that. "'FN,' huh? I'm calling you Finn. That all right?"

Finn couldn't help smiling. "Yeah, I like that."

Poe flew the TIE fighter towards Jakku. He told Finn that they had to find his droid, BB-8. But as they drew closer to the planet, the First Order Star Destroyer regained control of its weapons.

FIRST ORDER STAR DESTROYER (FINALIZER)

The *Finalizer* is a First Order Star Destroyer with a dagger-shaped shadow similar to the Imperial battleships of yesteryear.

The Star Destroyer fired on the TIE, sending the small fighter spiralling towards Jakku's sandy surface.

Finn managed to eject before the ship hit the ground, but there was no sign of Poe. Finn could find only the pilot's flight jacket.

Suddenly, the crashed TIE fighter began sinking into the dune beneath it. It had landed on quicksand!

Finn didn't want to leave Poe behind, but if he didn't run, he would certainly be pulled into the sinking sand.

Reluctantly, he fled from the crashed ship, carrying Poe's jacket.

Once he was safe, Finn looked around. He had no idea where he was. Sand stretched in every direction, and the sun was beating down on him. Unless he found water and shelter, he wouldn't last very long.

Finn removed his armour and used Poe's jacket to shield himself from the heat of the sun. After walking for hours, he spotted a small outpost in the distance. He was saved!

Finn ran to the outpost and collapsed in a trough of water, drinking greedily.

Meanwhile, two of Unkar's thugs were attacking Rey and trying to steal BB-8!

After years of living alone in the desert, Rey knew how to take care of herself. She quickly knocked out the thugs and spun around, looking for any other threats.

As she turned, she saw a young man next to a trough of water, looking at BB-8 in shock.

The young man was Finn. He couldn't believe he had found Poe's droid. Finn tried to explain to Rey as quickly as he could that he knew BB-8's master and the droid was carrying a map for the Resistance.

"So you're with the Resistance?" Rey asked.

Finn stopped.

He didn't want Rey to know that he had been a stormtrooper.

"Yes," he lied.

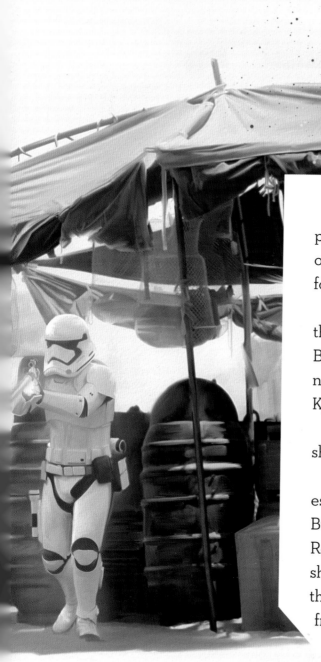

Suddenly, a blaster bolt flew past. Finn turned and saw a platoon of stormtroopers heading straight for them. They needed to run. Now!

Shot after shot whizzed past them. The stormtroopers wanted BB-8, and they would stop at nothing to capture the droid for Kylo Ren.

"We can't outrun them!" Finn shouted to Rey.

Finn was right. They couldn't escape the stormtroopers on foot. But they might be able to in a ship! Rey led them towards a nearby shipyard, desperate for any ship that could get them far, far away from the First Order soldiers.

Finn, Rey and BB-8 ran towards a sleek new ship that was sure to get them off Jakku. But before they could climb on board, First Order TIE fighters opened fire from the sky and destroyed the ship.

They took the next available ship they found. It was a hunk of junk, but Rey knew that it belonged to Unkar Plutt.

Rey jumped into the cockpit, and Finn sat in the gunner's chair. "You ever fly this thing?" Finn asked.

Rey was a good pilot, but she had never flown a ship that large. "I can do this. I can do this," she repeated to herself.

Rey concentrated, then flipped a few switches. The engines roared to life, and Rey breathed a sigh of relief.

"Stay low and put up the shields - if they work!" Finn suggested.

Finn watched as the stormtroopers on the ground disappeared from view. But First Order TIE fighters were waiting for them in the air.

Two enemy ships screamed past them and started firing. A blast rocked them as Finn tried his best to fire back.

"We need cover, quick!" he yelled.

"We're about to get some," Rey replied. She banked hard and turned the ship towards the fields of wreckage out in the desert.

MILLENNIUM FALCON An extensively modified Corellian light freighter, the *Millennium Falcon* is a legend in smuggling circles and coveted by many as the fastest hunk of junk in the galaxy.

Rey weaved between the crashed ships, trying to lose the TIE fighters.

Finn managed to shoot down one of the enemy ships, but there was still one TIE close on their tail.

"The cannon's stuck in forward position. I can't move it!" Finn yelled.

Another blast rocked their ship. Rey needed to find better cover. She spotted the hollowed-out hull of a crashed Super Star Destroyer. If she could fly *through* the big ship, maybe they could lose the TIE fighter – if Rey could keep them from crashing themselves.

When Finn saw that Rey was flying towards the Super Star Destroyer, he couldn't believe it.

"*Are we really doing this?*" he shouted.

But Rey had made up her mind. She flew into one of the Super Star Destroyer's exhaust ports, with the TIE fighter close behind.

Debris pelted both ships, but Rey kept focused on the opening at the other end of the Super Star Destroyer.

They zoomed closer and closer, and then Rey shouted: "Get ready!"

"For what?" Finn cried.

In reply, Rey yanked the controls of the ship to the right and flew out into the bright sunlight. Then she cut the engines, flipping the ship around so Finn's gunner turret was pointed right at the TIE fighter.

Finn took the hint and fired. The enemy ship exploded in a hail of sparks!

Now that the skies were clear, Rey flew into space and away from the First Order troops.

Finn climbed down from the gunner's seat and ran to Rey. "How did you do that? That was amazing!"

Rey smiled. "That last shot was dead-on. You got him with one blast!"

Finn's excitement started to vanish when he realised what they had to do next. Rey thought he was a member of the Resistance. She would expect him to know how to get to the Resistance base.

Somehow, he had to get BB-8 to tell him the location of the base without Rey finding out.

Lucky for Finn, their escape from Jakku had damaged the ship's motivator. A puff of steam burst from the grate beneath them. Rey jumped down to inspect the damage.

"How bad is it?" Finn shouted down to her.

"If we want to live? Not good." Rey immediately began fixing the broken motivator.

And Finn began talking BB-8 into revealing the location of the Resistance base.

Kylo Ren was furious.

Once again, the map to Luke Skywalker had slipped through his fingers.

Kylo went to his quarters to think. There he knelt before his most treasured possession – the lost mask of Darth Vader. Vader had been a powerful Sith Lord and the father of Luke Skywalker. Kylo spoke into the silence.

"Forgive me. I am so close to finding Skywalker. I can sense it. I will finish what you started," he promised. "I will find him and, in your name, kill him."

Later, one of Kylo's officers briefed him on the droid's disappearance.

"It escaped capture aboard a stolen Corellian YT model freighter."

"The droid stole a freighter?" Kylo asked, his patience wearing thin.

"Not exactly, sir," the lieutenant said. "It had help. We believe FN-2187 may have been—"

Kylo ignited his lightsaber in rage.

The lieutenant continued bravely. "The two were accompanied by a girl."

"What girl?" demanded Kylo. He would not let the map elude him a third time.

Kylo's master would hardly tolerate another failure . . .

Rey had almost finished repairing the ship's motivator, but Finn had not been as successful at getting BB-8 to tell him the location of the Resistance base.

As Rey reached for another tool, she asked the question Finn had been dreading. "So where's your base?"

Finn panicked. "Tell her, BB-8. Go ahead. It's OK."

BB-8 paused, then beeped obligingly.

"The Ileenium system?" Rey repeated.

"Yeah," Finn said. "Let's get there as fast as we can."

As if in response, every part of the ship suddenly lost power.

"Someone's locked on to us," Rey said, trying to hide her fear. "All controls are overridden."

The pair ran to the cockpit and looked out. A massive ship loomed above them, pulling them into its cargo bay.

"What do we do?" Rey asked. "There must be *something* . . ."

A thud rumbled through the freighter. They were now docked inside the big cargo ship.

With no other options, Finn, Rey and BB-8 hid beneath the floor grating, hoping to take the intruders by surprise.

From their hiding spot, Rey, Finn and BB-8 heard the ship's ramp lower.

"Here they come," Finn whispered.

Two figures stepped aboard. They immediately began looking through the ship and, within moments, found the trio's hiding place. It was as if they had known exactly where to look.

To their surprise, the two figures were not stormtroopers – just an old man and a Wookiee.

"Where'd you find this ship?" the man asked.

"Niima Outpost," Rey replied.

"Who had it? Ducain?"

"I stole it from Unkar Plutt. He stole it from the Irving Boys, who stole it from Ducain."

"Who stole it from me!" the man finished. "You tell him Han Solo just stole back the *Millennium Falcon* for good."

He turned to his Wookiee companion.

"Chewie . . . we're home."

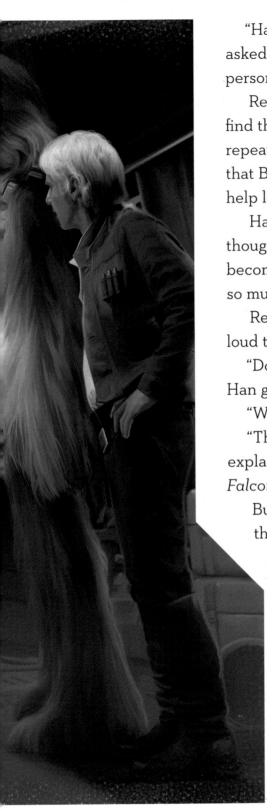

"Han Solo? The Rebellion general?" Rey asked. They couldn't have found a better person to help them if they had tried!

Rey quickly explained that they had to find the Resistance as soon as possible. Rey repeated what Finn had told her on Jakku: that BB-8 was carrying a map that would help lead to Luke Skywalker.

Han seemed reluctant to help them, though. He didn't know if he was ready to become a hero again. He had already lost so much.

Rey continued to argue with Han until a loud thud echoed through the *Falcon*.

"Don't tell me a rathtar's gotten loose . . ." Han groaned.

"What's a rathtar?" Rey asked.

"They're big and dangerous," Han explained gruffly. He led them out of the *Falcon* to check on the beasts.

But it wasn't Han's fearsome cargo making the racket. The Guavian Death Gang had broken into Han's ship. Han owed the gang money, and they were there to collect.

"Get below deck until I say so," Han told Rey and Finn. He motioned to the droid.

"He'll stay with me. When I get rid of the gang, you can have him back and be on your way."

Then he and Chewie took BB-8 and left to confront the gang.

GUAVIAN DEATH GANG The security soldiers of the Guavian Death Gang wear high-impact armour that makes them stand out among other deadly criminals.

But when he reached them, Han saw that the Guavian Death Gang weren't alone. They had brought Kanjiklub with them. Han had taken money from both gangs to hunt down the rathtars, and they wanted their money back. Now.

"Guys, you're all going to get what I promised," Han said, turning on the charm. "Have I ever not delivered for you before?"

"Twice," the leader of Kanjiklub replied. "Nowhere left for you to hide."

BB-8 cowered against Han's leg as the men raised their guns.

"That BB unit . . ." the Guavian Death Gang leader said suddenly. "The First Order is looking for one just like it. And two fugitives."

From the hull of the cargo ship, Rey tried to come up with an escape plan. She looked at the video monitors and suddenly got an idea.

"If we close the blast doors in that corridor, we can trap both gangs!"

Quickly, Rey went to work resetting the door fuses.

But as Rey crossed two wires, all the lights inside the cargo ship went out.

"Oh, no," Rey said, going pale. "Wrong fuses." Instead of closing the blast doors, Rey had opened the rathtars' cages and the ferocious beasts were free!

Han and Chewie took advantage of the confusion to take down a few gang members.

"Cover me!" Han shouted to Chewie. "I'll get to the *Falcon*."

Rey and Finn were also trying to get back to the *Falcon*. They raced through corridors, trying to find a way out that wasn't blocked by the terrifying rathtars.

Suddenly, the pair turned a corner and found themselves face to face with one of the beasts.

The creature immediately reached out a long slimy tentacle and pulled Finn down the hallway at lightning speed.

"Finn!" Rey cried out.

She knew she could never keep up with the rathtar on foot. Instead, she ran to a control panel, where she could follow the rathtar on the video monitors. As she watched it slither through doorway after doorway, Rey got an idea.

She held her hand over the blast door control, waiting for just the right moment, and then – SLAM! Rey closed the blast door right on top of the rathtar, freeing Finn.

Rey helped Finn to his feet and together they ran back to the Falcon.

While the battle raged on, Han and Chewie were getting closer to the Millennium Falcon. But as they made their way towards the ship, a blast hit Chewie in the shoulder!

Han quickly grabbed Chewie's bowcaster and fired at the oncoming gang members, managing to hold them off long enough for everyone to get aboard the Falcon.

"Move it!" Han shouted to Rey and Finn. He pointed to Rey. "You shut the hatch behind us."

He turned to Finn. "You take care of Chewie."

Together, they raced up the ramp and into the Falcon. Finn led Chewie back to the medbay while Rey and Han took their seats in the cockpit.

"Watch the thrust, we're gonna jump to lightspeed," Han told Rey.

"From inside a hangar? Is that even possible?" Rey asked.

"I never ask that question until after I've done it."

Together, they prepared the *Falcon* for lightspeed.

"Come on, baby. Don't let me down," Han said quietly, then flipped a switch.

Nothing happened.

"What?" Han cried.

But Rey calmly pressed a button.

"Compressor," she explained.

Han flipped the switch for lightspeed one more time, and instantly the *Falcon* shot into hyperspace.

GENERAL LEIA ORGANA Unable to muster the help she needed from the New Republic, Leia Organa – ever vigilant against the return of darkness to the galaxy – struck out on her own as the leader of the Resistance opposed to the rise of the First Order.

At the Resistance base, General Leia Organa was waiting for any information about the missing map.

A young officer named Brance ran to find her and deliver the latest news. "General, the Jakku village was wiped out. Lor San Tekka was killed." He bowed his head.

"If they get to Luke first," Leia said grimly, "we don't have a chance."

Brance went on to say that Poe was missing and there was no word from BB-8.

C-3PO A fastidious and worry-prone protocol droid, C-3PO longs for more peaceful times, but his continued service to Princess Leia keeps him on the front lines of galactic conflict.

"Never underestimate a droid," Leia reminded Brance before he walked away.

Leia then turned to her faithful protocol droid, C-3PO.

"Locate BB-8 immediately," she told him. "You know what to do."

"Yes, General, of course," C-3PO replied. "The tracking system!"

STARKILLER BASE is an ice planet converted into a stronghold for the First Order and armed with a fiercely destructive new weapon capable of destroying entire star systems.

Far away, on a planet covered in ice and snow, Kylo Ren and General Hux, the leader of the First Order troops, were brought before their master: Supreme Leader Snoke.

"The droid will soon be in the hands of the Resistance. This will give our enemy the means to locate Skywalker," thundered the towering figure of cold grey flesh.

"I do have a proposition," Hux said. "The weapon. It is ready."

"Good," Snoke replied. "Oversee preparations."

Hux bowed gratefully and left.

Snoke then turned to face Kylo.

"There has been an awakening in the Force," the dark figure warned. Kylo would have an important part to play in the coming conflict.

"Had Lord Vader not succumbed to emotion at that critical moment, there would be no threat of Skywalker's return today," cautioned Snoke.

Kylo's master leaned closer. "You will face a test first. One neither of us could foresee. The droid we seek is aboard the *Millennium Falcon*, once again piloted by Han Solo."

"My allegiance is with you. No one will stand in our way." Kylo raised his eyes to meet Snoke's. "No one."

Back on board the *Falcon*, Han was examining BB-8's map.

"Ever since Luke disappeared, people have been looking for him."

"Why'd he leave?" Rey asked.

Han explained that Luke had been training the next generation of Jedi.

"One boy – an apprentice turned against him and destroyed it all."

Luke, overcome with guilt, had walked away from everything and everyone.

Han agreed to help them get to the Resistance base. But they had to make one stop first . . .

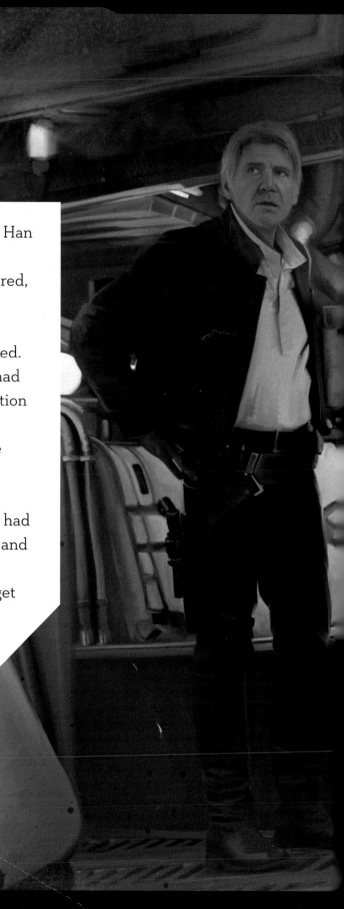

The *Falcon* exited hyperspace above a lush planet called Takodana. The landscape was covered in wide forests and glistening lakes. Rey had never seen so much greenery in all her life!

"What are we doing here?" Finn asked. They were still a long way from the Resistance base.

"Getting help," Han replied. "You'll see."

Han landed the *Falcon* outside a large stone structure that looked like an ancient castle. While the outside of the building was impressive, it was the interior that made Rey and Finn gasp in amazement.

The great hall was filled with aliens and humans from every corner of the galaxy.

"Haaaaaan Solo!" came a joyful cry from somewhere in the centre of the crowded room.

Immediately, everyone fell silent and turned towards a short golden alien. She was wearing simple clothes and a giant pair of goggles that magnified her eyes into big blue spheres.

"Hiya, Maz," Han said with a crooked smile.

But Maz's large eyes failed to notice a First Order spy hidden among her guests. As soon as the spy saw Finn and his friends, she sent word to Kylo Ren.

Maz provided Han and his friends with food and drink while Han filled her in on their mission.

Rey was excited to soon reach the Resistance, but Finn was ready to go his own way. He didn't want to be exposed to the entire Resistance as the liar he was, and he didn't want any part in fighting the First Order. It was too powerful. He knew first-hand.

Maz told Finn where he could find work on a departing shuttle. But Rey couldn't understand why he wanted to leave.

"You're part of this fight. We both are."

"I'm not who you think I am," Finn said sadly. "I'm a stormtrooper. I'm not a hero."

Rey couldn't believe her ears. How could the kind and brave man she had spent the past few days with possibly be a stormtrooper?

Lost in thought, Rey wandered through the vast hallways of the castle.

Suddenly, Rey stopped in front of a doorway. A dark stairway beyond seemed to call to her. She was drawn down and down into a cluttered basement room. In the centre of the room was an old wooden box. As Rey approached the box, her mind was overwhelmed with visions of Kylo Ren, the First Order and the destruction that was to come.

Then she heard a voice, both familiar and strange.

"I'll come back, sweetheart. I promise."

MAZ KANATA This colourful alien holds court in an ancient castle on Takodana, where she reigns as the most knowledgeable smuggler around, with centuries of experience. She has an uncanny knack for sensing the shifting tides of fortune in the galaxy.

As quickly as the vision had begun, it stopped. But Rey was no longer alone. Maz was standing patiently behind her.

"What was that?" Rey demanded.

"It's the Force," Maz replied.

Maz tried to explain the destiny that awaited Rey, but Rey was not ready to hear her. Not yet.

Rey fled the small room, looking for somewhere she could be alone.

But across the galaxy, Rey's vision was already coming true. General Hux stood before an army of stormtroopers, making a grand speech.

"Today," he began, "is the end."

The First Order had finally completed work on the Starkiller. Now they would show the galaxy the power of their mighty weapon.

Hux gave the command and a blast of destruction burned its way across the galaxy, obliterating the entire solar system that held the New Republic Senate. There was now no one left but the Resistance to stand against the First Order.

Even on Takodana, Han, Chewie and Finn saw the beam from the Starkiller reaching across the stars.

"The First Order. They've gone and destroyed it," Finn said in disbelief. Then his mind snapped to something even more important to him. "Where's Rey?"

"Rey is where she needs to be," Maz assured him. She led the trio back to the basement room where Rey had experienced her vision. Maz opened the wooden box and pulled out a lightsaber.

"Where'd you get that?" asked Han.

"Long story," Maz responded. "A good one - for later."

Then she handed the lightsaber to Finn.

A terrifying rumble shook the castle to its foundations. The spy had brought Kylo Ren and his soldiers to Takodana. Transports filled the sky as stormtroopers began landing nearby and firing on the castle.

Han knew they had to get back to the *Falcon*. But first they had to find Rey and BB-8! Han, Chewie and Finn fought their way outside, dodging blaster fire.

Meanwhile, Rey was busy avoiding stormtroopers herself.

"Keep going!" she shouted to BB-8. "I'll fight 'em off!"

Rey managed to take down a few stormtroopers with her blaster. But then she heard the menacing hum of Kylo Ren's lightsaber. He had found her.

"Tell me, girl," Kylo growled. "Where is the droid I seek?"

Rey fired her blaster at the shadowy figure, but Kylo deflected the shots with his red lightsaber.

Kylo drew closer and closer to Rey, reaching out with the Force to read her mind. As he searched her thoughts, Kylo discovered his goal was nearer than he had realised.

"You've seen it. The map – it's in your mind."

Kylo wouldn't need the droid after all. He grabbed Rey and took her back towards his ship.

Han, Chewie and Finn were slowly getting closer and closer to the *Falcon*. But it was tough going.

Finn ignited the lightsaber and used its bright blade to deflect fire from the attacking soldiers.

From behind them, a stormtrooper with an electrostaff charged right at Finn. Sparks flew as the staff connected with Finn's saber.

Finn moved quickly, taking out the soldier and two other troopers nearby. But for each enemy Han, Finn or Chewie stopped, there were two more to take his place.

HAN SOLO The exploits of Han Solo are legendary. He's a famed smuggler, captain of the *Millennium Falcon*, and a hero of the Rebel Alliance. As the galaxy teeters towards war, Solo once again finds himself at the centre of the action.

"You see a way out of this, pal?" Han muttered to Chewie.

As if in answer, a black X-wing streaked across the sky above them, followed by an entire squadron of Resistance ships. They were saved! Soon Resistance soldiers were flooding the battlefield, turning the tide against the First Order.

CHEWBACCA
First mate and copilot to Han Solo, Chewbacca has loyally stood by his captain's side through the twisting fortunes of a galaxy in turmoil.

Now Finn just had to get to Rey. He raced through the woods, fighting off anyone who stood in his way.

But as Finn walked into a clearing, he saw that he was too late. He watched helplessly as Kylo Ren forced Rey on board the First Order transport and flew away.

The remaining First Order troops retreated behind Kylo's ship.
As silence fell over the battlefield, one last Resistance ship landed.
The shuttle doors opened and out walked General Leia Organa.

Han approached her slowly and answered the question she didn't
even have to ask.

"I saw him. He was here."

Han, Chewie, Finn and BB-8 boarded the *Falcon* and followed the
Resistance fighters back to their secret base. They had much to discuss.
With the New Republic all but destroyed, the Resistance would need to
move quickly if it was going to have any hope of stopping the First Order.

RESISTANCE X-WING
The modern incarnation of a classic design, the Incom T-70 X-wing fighter is the signature combat craft of the Resistance forces in their fight against the First Order.

The Starkiller required a massive amount of energy to recharge its ray. It would take time before the First Order could target another system – time the Resistance would use to come up with a plan.

When the *Falcon* landed, BB-8 raced down the exit ramp towards the black X-wing. The little droid was beeping wildly. Finn couldn't understand what had gotten into BB-8, until the pilot of the X-wing took off his helmet.

"Poe!" Finn cried in disbelief.

Poe had survived the crash on Jakku and was once again flying for the Resistance. Finn was so happy to see his friend. He would need all the help he could get to rescue Rey. He was ashamed that he had almost left before their mission was complete.

Now that BB-8 was back at the Resistance base, he had two other friends to visit.

C-3PO and R2-D2 had been helping Skywalkers fight villains since before the first Empire rose to power. After decades of service, both of them were a little worse for the wear. C-3PO had been rebuilt more times than he cared to remember, and R2-D2 reserved his energy by staying in low-power mode.

Ever since Luke had left, R2 hadn't spoken to anyone.

BB-8 beeped hopefully at his friend, but R2 didn't respond.

R2-D2 A loyal and dependable astromech droid well equipped for starship repair and computer interface. Even after decades of service R2-D2 continues to be full of surprises.

Light-years away, Kylo Ren had imprisoned Rey in a cell on the Starkiller base.

"Tell me about the droid," Kylo demanded. "He's carrying a section of a navigational chart. We have the rest, but we need the last piece."

Rey stayed silent, struggling against her restraints.

"I know you've seen the map," Kylo said. "I can take whatever I want."

Rey felt Kylo reach into her mind with the Force and search her thoughts. But she pushed back against him. She focused on the connection between them.

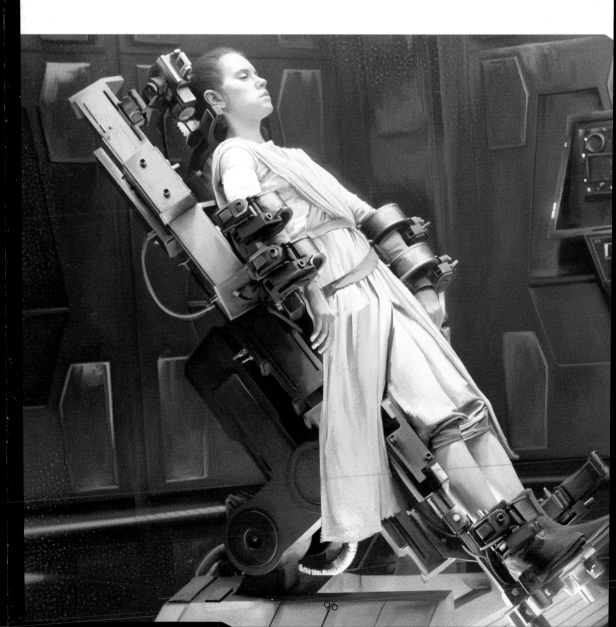

Suddenly, Rey was flooded with images and emotions from Kylo's mind. She sensed anger and pain but most of all fear.

Kylo quickly pulled away from Rey and left the cell. He was shocked and confused by her power.

Rey could still feel the Force flowing through her. She wondered if she could use it again. Addressing the guard at her cell door, she spoke in a commanding voice: "You will remove these restraints and leave this cell with the door open."

To her surprise, the guard unlocked her shackles and headed out of the cell.

"And you will drop your weapon," Rey added quickly. After he had gone, she picked up his discarded blaster and ran from the cell.

Back at the Resistance base, the team was planning its attack on the Starkiller.

"We've just received word," Leia said. "They're charging the weapon again now. Our system is their next target."

Quickly, they finalised their mission.

Han, Chewie and Finn would land on the enemy base and take down the weapon's shields from the inside. Then Poe and his team of pilots would fly in and destroy the oscillator. The oscillator was a crucial part of the Starkiller that kept it from overheating and imploding.

Finn also planned to rescue Rey from Kylo Ren. It would be risky, but Finn refused to leave her behind.

As Han, Chewie and Finn approached the Starkiller base in the *Millennium Falcon*, Han explained that the base's shields kept out anything travelling slower than lightspeed.

"We're gonna make our landing approach at lightspeed?" Finn cried. How would they slow down in time to avoid crashing into the planet's surface?

But Han and Chewie weren't worried. Working together, the pair exited lightspeed just inside the base's shields.

The *Falcon* sped towards the ground and skidded to a halt on the planet's snowy surface.

As the trio left the *Falcon*, they could see a great beam of light extending into the sky. The weapon was draining all the power from a nearby star. Once the star was extinguished, the weapon would be ready to fire. They had to destroy the Starkiller before that happened.

"The flooding tunnels are over that ridge," Finn said. "We'll get in that way." Finn led Han and Chewie to the entrance of the tunnels and helped them get inside.

Han, Chewie and Finn crept through the corridors, taking out any stormtroopers who stood in their way.

Then Finn spotted Captain Phasma. His old commander would know exactly how to get to the shields – and how to take them down!

Finn nodded slowly to Chewie. The Wookiee leaped out and grabbed the unsuspecting captain.

"Remember me?" Finn asked fiercely.

The captain recognised him immediately. "FN-2187!"

"Not anymore," he replied. "You're taking orders from *Finn* now."

Phasma had no choice; she was forced to help them take down the Starkiller's shields. Now they just had to find Rey!

Nearby, Rey was still looking for a way off the Starkiller base. At the end of a long walkway, she saw a hangar bay full of TIE fighters. With a ship, she could fly away from the base and find the Resistance. The only problem was the platoon of stormtroopers between her and the hangar.

There was no way she could fight all of them. But before Rey could decide what to do next, she heard a second platoon coming towards her.

Undetected, Rey climbed under the walkway and held on tightly to the smooth wall below. She would never be able to get to the hangar. But she might be able to get to the base's surface instead . . .

Once they received the message that the Starkiller's shields were down, Poe and his fellow pilots entered the planet's atmosphere and started their attack.

"Hit the target dead centre, as many runs as we can get," Poe ordered. "Let's light it up!"

Finn heard the X-wing's blasts as they connected with the Starkiller. They had to find Rey soon. Han, Chewie and Finn ran towards the base's prison cells – and right into Rey!

"What are you doing here?" Rey exclaimed when she saw her friends.

"We came back for you," Finn said.

Rey thanked Finn with a tight hug, and together they ran to find the *Falcon*.

But when they reached the surface of the base, they saw that the X-wings still hadn't destroyed the oscillator. The team knew they had to help.

"My friend here has a bag full of explosives," Han said, gesturing to Chewie. "Let's use 'em."

Han and Chewie began planting explosives around the interior of the oscillator structure while Rey and Finn kept watch for stormtroopers.

Han was setting the last charge when he saw a figure in a black robe heading his way. It could only be Kylo Ren. But instead of raising his blaster, Han stepped out of the shadows and called to Kylo using his real name. "Ben!"

Kylo spun around to face Han. "I've been waiting for this day for a long time."

So had Han. Ever since Kylo had fallen to the dark side of the Force, Han had been waiting for his son to return to him. The loss of Kylo had even driven Han and Leia apart. Han begged his son to come home.

But Kylo would not listen. He extended his lightsaber and silenced his father forever.

Chewie cried out in horror as Finn and Rey watched helplessly from above. They still had a mission to complete. Chewie managed to set off the explosives, but a squad of stormtroopers separated him from Finn and Rey as they all ran for the planet's surface.

From inside his X-wing cockpit, Poe saw the glow of the detonations rocking the oscillator.

"Hit the target hard!" Poe called to the other pilots. "Give it everything you've got!"

Poe raced towards the damaged oscillator and fired at the burning wreck. The ground surrounding it began to buckle and collapse as the weapon overheated. With one more blast, Poe destroyed the oscillator in a fiery explosion.

Finn and Rey heard the oscillator's destruction as they ran across the snowy planet, back towards the *Falcon*.

But Kylo Ren was close behind them. He wasn't going to let them escape without a fight. Finn and Rey realised they couldn't outrun the First Order warrior, so they turned to face him.

Rey raised her blaster, but Kylo used the Force to throw her to the ground.

Before Kylo could attack him, too, Finn drew the lightsaber Maz had given him.

Kylo sneered. "That weapon . . . is mine."

"Come get it," Finn replied.

Finn ran and lunged at Kylo. Sparks flew as their lightsabers connected.

Kylo snarled and took a step back, then thrust his fiery blade close to Finn's chest. Finn lifted his lightsaber and managed to block the attack just in time. But Kylo kept swinging, faster and faster.

Finn used every ounce of his training to fight Kylo, but it wasn't enough. Only someone with a strong connection to the Force could defeat a warrior such as Kylo.

With a mighty blow, Kylo knocked Finn to the ground, badly wounding him.

Kylo used the Force to pull Finn's lightsaber out of his grasp. The weapon flew towards Kylo . . .

. . . then sped right past him and into Rey's waiting hand.

Kylo stared at Rey in disbelief. "It is *you*," he breathed.

Rey had no idea what he meant. But she didn't care. She ignited the lightsaber and charged.

Her blue lightsaber crashed against Kylo's burning red blade. She felt the Force surging through her, showing her where he would strike next.

"I don't want to kill you," Kylo said, dodging a swipe from Rey's saber.

Rey almost laughed. "Don't you?"

"You need a teacher," Kylo insisted. "I can show you the ways of the Force."

"You're a monster," Rey snarled, forcing Kylo to leap back from her flashing blade.

Rey could tell Kylo was growing tired, so she pressed her advantage. Suddenly, the ground began shaking. The destruction of the Starkiller weapon was tearing apart the base. With another shudder, the forest floor beside them fell away, creating a giant cliff.

Rey intensified her attacks, her anger rising with every blow.

Her blade cut across Kylo's face before connecting with his saber hilt. Kylo's weapon flew into the snow and he fell to the ground, panting in exhaustion.

Rey realised she could end everything. She could destroy Kylo for good.

With a rumble, the ground between them split. A great gulf opened, separating Rey from Kylo. He was beyond her reach, but she had defeated him for now.

Rey ran back to Finn and knelt at his side. His wound was deep and he needed help right away.

She glanced back at Kylo. His men had found him and were leading him to an escape shuttle. Kylo would live to fight another day.

Rey held Finn tightly as she tried to think of a plan. She had to get them to the *Falcon*, but she couldn't carry him by herself.

As Rey shivered next to Finn in the snow, they were suddenly flooded with light. It was Chewbacca! He had flown the *Millennium Falcon* to them.

Chewie helped Rey carry Finn on board. Then she and Chewie took their seats in the cockpit and set a course for the Resistance base. Behind them, the Starkiller collapsed in a burst of light and heat. The Resistance had destroyed the weapon once and for all!

When the *Falcon* reached the base, Rey saw that a small crowd had gathered to meet them. Poe, C-3PO, BB-8 and Leia were waiting on the landing pad.

When Rey left the ship, she went straight to Leia. Rey had no words to express how sorry she was, but fortunately Leia didn't need words. The older woman wrapped Rey in a hug. Although they both mourned Han's loss, they took comfort in the fact that the Resistance was safe.

With the Starkiller destroyed, the Resistance could once again focus on its original mission: finding Luke Skywalker.

"Kylo Ren said that BB-8's map is the last piece?" Poe asked Rey.

Rey nodded. "The First Order has the rest of it, from the archive of the Empire."

Without that part of the map, they still had no way of finding Luke.

Just then, an excited beeping burst through the silence.

"Artoo!" C-3PO said happily. "I haven't seen you this functional since—"

R2-D2 interrupted his friend, explaining that he had the missing map piece.

R2 projected the portion of the map he had been storing for decades, and BB-8 projected his piece. The two images fit perfectly, uniting to form a complete map!

"Oh, my stars!" C-3PO cried. "That's it!" He laid a gentle hand on R2's metal dome. "My dear friend, how I've missed you!"

Everyone erupted in cheers. With Luke on their side, their next confrontation with the First Order would be very different. It was Rey's task to find him.

Chewie prepared the *Falcon* for flight while Rey said goodbye to Finn in the medical bay. She hated leaving him while he was still recovering, but she knew her mission couldn't wait.

When Rey reached the landing pad, Leia was waiting for her. She hugged Rey and gave her a parting blessing:

"May the Force be with you."

Rey and Chewie flew the *Falcon* to the planet marked on their map: Ahch-To. The planet's beautiful blue waters were dotted with islands.

Rey landed the *Falcon* at the base of the tallest island. A rugged mountain path led to a small clearing near the summit.

When Rey reached the top, an old man in a brown robe was waiting for her. Luke Skywalker was strong in the Force and had sensed her arrival.

Rey handed the Jedi Master his lightsaber. She didn't know what the future held. But she did know her adventure had only just begun . . .